This enchanted book belongs to:

_____

_____

your name goes here!

North Parade
Publishing Ltd
4 North Parade | Bath UK | BA1 1LF
+44(0) 1225 310107
www.nppbooks.co.uk

The Enchanted Tree

Illustrated by Ela Jarzabek

For my Parents x E.J.

There was a terrible drought in Africa. No rain had fallen for over a year, and as far as the eye could see, the land was hard, and scorched.

Desperately the animals searched for food.

One day, venturing as far as his weak legs would carry him, Lion came upon an enchanted tree. Its branches bowed beneath the weight of lush green leaves and succulent fruits; there were apples, oranges, peaches, mangoes, plums, melons, figs, and apricots.

Lion's mouth watered; he licked his lips, and drew closer to the magic tree.

Suddenly, he was thrown backwards by an invisible force, and could not go any farther.

Hungry and disappointed, Lion returned to the other animals to tell them what he'd seen.

"We must go to Grandmother Koko!" said Tortoise at once. "She will know how to reach the magic tree, and then we will all be able to eat!"

"No, no, no!" said Elephant, impatiently. "Lion must go back, and take me with him. I will be able to break the invisible force and reach the fruit."

"We should all go," said Giraffe. She was worried that Elephant would break the magic spell, and take all the fruit for himself.

And so the animals all set off together; Lion in front with Elephant...

...and Tortoise bringing up the rear.

Finally, they reached the Enchanted Tree.

Elephant pawed the ground determinedly, and galloped towards it.

Suddenly, he was thrown backwards by an invisible force, and could not get any closer.

"We should all try!" said Giraffe, sensibly.

Lion, Elephant, Giraffe, Zebra, Hyena, Ostrich, Baboon, and Rhino all stood together, shoulder to shoulder.

Tortoise hurried forward to take his place.

"Not you!" said Hyena, meanly. "You're too small!"

With that, they dashed towards the Enchanted Tree, and were all thrown backwards, just as Lion and Elephant had been before.

Tortoise stifled a giggle.

"I will go to Grandmother Koko," he said. "She will know how to reach the magic tree; then we will all be able to eat."

"You're too slow!" said Lion. "I will go myself!"

And off he went.

Lion told Grandmother Koko all about the Enchanted Tree.

"I have heard of this tree," said wise Grandmother Koko. "It is called **'Uwungelema,'** and if you want the fruit to fall you must call out its name!"

"**Uwungelema!**" repeated Lion.

He thanked Grandmother Koko, and hurried back the way he had come.

In his haste, he overlooked an anthill in his path.

Crash! He stumbled and fell, and the name flew out of his head!

Hungry and frustrated, Lion trooped back to the other animals, and told them what Grandmother Koko had told him.

Try as he might, he could not recall the name to make the fruits fall.

"I will go to Grandmother Koko!" said Elephant. "I won't forget the name!"

And off he went.

"It is called 'Uwungelema,'" said Grandmother Koko, "and if you want the fruits to fall, you must call out its name!"

"Uwungelema!" repeated Elephant. He thanked Grandmother Koko, and hurried back towards the Enchanted Tree.

He saw the anthill, and rushed on...

In his haste he overlooked a giant creeper in his path.

Crash! He became tangled, and fell, and the name flew out of his head!

The other animals were waiting for Elephant beside the Enchanted Tree.

"Do you remember the name?" they cried.

Elephant shook his head sadly; try as he might, he could not remember the name that would make the fruits fall.

"I will go to Grandmother Koko!" said Giraffe. "I won't forget the name!"

And off she went.

"It is called '**Uwungelema,**'" said Grandmother Koko, "and if you want the fruits to fall, you must call out its name!"

"**Uwungelema!**" repeated Giraffe.

She thanked Grandmother Koko, and hurried back towards the Enchanted Tree.

She saw the **anthill**, and the **creeper**, and rushed on...

In her haste she overlooked a snake in her path.

"Hissssssssssss!" said the snake.

Giraffe gasped, and the name flew out of her head!

Hungry and frustrated, she trooped back to the Enchanted Tree where the other animals were waiting for her.

"Do you remember the name?" they cried.

Giraffe shook her head sadly; try as she might, she could not recall the name to make the fruits fall.

"I will go to Grandmother Koko!" said Zebra. "I won't forget the name!"

And off she went.

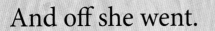

"It is called '**Uwungelema**,'" said Grandmother Koko, "and if you want the fruits to fall, you must call out its name!"

"**Uwungelema!**" repeated Zebra.

She thanked Grandmother Koko, and hurried back to the Enchanted Tree.

She saw the **anthill**, and the **creeper**, and the **snake**, and rushed on...

In her haste she overlooked a thorn in her path.

"**Ouch!**" cried Zebra, and the name flew out of her head!

"Do you remember the name?" the animals cried, when Zebra finally reached the Enchanted Tree.

She shook her head sadly; try as she might, she could not recall the name to make the fruits fall.

Next went **Hyena**, then **Ostrich**, followed by **Baboon**, and lastly **Rhino**.

Try as they might, none of them could remember the name to make the fruits fall.

"What will we do?" the animals asked, gazing longingly at the dangling fruits.

"Please let me go!" begged Tortoise.

"I won't forget the name!"

Finally, the animals agreed, and off Tortoise went.

"It is called '**Uwungelema**,'" said Grandmother Koko, "and if you want the fruits to fall, you must call out its name."

"**Uwungelema!**" repeated Tortoise.

He thanked Grandmother Koko, and started back towards the Enchanted Tree.

He saw the **anthill**, he saw the **creeper**, he saw the **snake**, and slowly but steadily, he plodded on...

He avoided the **scorpion** that distracted Hyena, he dodged the **log** that tripped Ostrich, and slowly but surely, he plodded on....

He sidestepped the **rocks** that made Baboon stumble, he missed the **branch** that thwarted Rhino, and slowly and carefully, he plodded on...

Eventually, Tortoise reached the Enchanted Tree.

The other animals were waiting for him there, gazing longingly at the dangling fruits.

"Do you remember the name?" they cried.

"**Uwungelema!**" yelled Tortoise.

Down fell the apples, oranges, peaches, mangoes, plums, melons, figs, and apricots, and in their places on the branches, many more appeared.

"We must all plant a seed!" said Tortoise, after the animals had eaten their fill.